Eboneigh
A Boss Christmas Tale
By: Kyeate

Eboneigh: A Boss Christmas Tale

Stay Connected

Facebook: Kyeate DaAuthor -Kyeate Holt-KyeWritez & Thingz

Instagram: KyeWritez

Twitter: Adjustnmykrown

Chapter 1
Eboneigh Scroo

The sounds coming from the money machines were music to my ears. Nothing and I meant nothing brought me joy but my money. If you had it rough like I did, then you would surely understand. Sitting in my office, I glanced over at the cameras that I had placed in the dressing rooms. Yes, I had cameras in just about every inch of my establishment.

I was the proud owner of Satin & Lace Dreams. My club stayed open twenty-four hours. We did a twenty-four-hour rotation so that everyone could get it in. Men loved to see ass while eating a nice lunch catered by the best in the city. On top of having the sexiest women working the stages and private rooms, you can get a good meal whether it was breakfast, lunch, or dinner. I put my all into my work because I birthed this shit myself. Nobody gave me shit, and I had to get it out of the mud.

Wrapping the rubber band around the grand that I just counted, I reached into my drawer and grabbed my bitch, Pearl. Standing to my feet, I fixed my fitted Gucci blazer and ran my hands down my 30-inch weave. When I was young and wilding out, I was into tattoos heavy. My ink covered my neck, and I even had a few tattoos on my face, which made motherfuckers turn they nose up at me. Nobody wanted to hire me, so it was only right I went into business for myself. Everything that graced and covered my cinnamon skin told a story.

Walking out of my office, the loud music blared through the speakers. My club was luxurious, and everything in it was white and gold. As I walked through, I felt my face change to the permanent mug that I always kept on it. I couldn't be smiling up in these bitches' faces. In no way was I their friend or into all that sisterly bonding shit.

It was Christmas Eve and 5:30 p.m. Granted, business was a little slow today with it being a fucking holiday, but the show must still go on.

I knew they whispered shit about me when I walked past the employees, but they knew to keep that shit cute because they weren't about to say that shit to my face.

"Aye yo, EB, where you going?" Bambino called out.

Bambino was my assistant. I ignored him and kept walking into the dressing room. The sight before me had me ready to knock a few hoes out when I walked into the room. As soon as they heard the door slam and noticed it was me, them hoes scattered like roaches when you turn the lights on.

"Don't fucking try to run now. Why the fuck are these chairs getting more action than the customers out there?" I spat.

"EB, it's fucking Christmas Eve. Ain't nobody in here, but the same lonely motherfuckers and the rest of the ballers with actual money are where we need to be, at home with our families. You can't be that hard up for cash," Marissa seethed.

She the only one that always tried me, and we have actually come to blows before. She was my top moneymaker.

"Excuse me. You want to be with your family on Christmas Eve, huh Marissa. Well, pack up your shit and get the fuck out of my club. I'm never hard up for cash, so you better watch what the fuck comes out of your mouth." I spat, walking up on her.

"You gone fire me on Christmas? Ain't nobody out there. Well, since I'm fired, bitch, I hope you die a slow miserable death, and then somebody burns your ass up along with all your money. Some of us do have children that look up to us, and spending the holiday with mine is more important," Marissa sassed and started to gather her things.

"If anybody else got a problem with being here, then take your ass out the door with her, but not before you give me my cut for the day," I yelled, pulling out pearl and placing it beside my hip.

"Where you going?" Bambino asked Marissa as she was about to walk out the door.

"EB's firing folks for wanting to spend the holiday with their families, ole mean ass bitch," she mugged me, and I did the same. Marissa walked out, and I noticed that Bambino followed her out, but that wasn't my concern.

Turning back around, I walked over to the vanity area and ran my fingers across the marble top.

"Who the fuck was on dusting duty this shift because this shit is nasty?" I asked. The other girls that were in the room hurried to dust the marble vanity tops.

I needed some hand sanitizer and fast. I walked over to the foam station, got me a squirt of sanitizer for my hands, and walked out of the dressing room. As I made my way to the front of the club, I noticed Marissa crying, and Bambino was smiling. He probably was fucking her ass.

My love life was nonexistent, and I didn't do relationships. That shit left a bad taste in my mouth. Love, family, and friendships, what was the purpose of the useless emotions that come from that?

Before heading to my office, I approached the bartender and held up my finger, meaning I wanted my special drink. Nodding her head, she moved around, making my drink. Bambino and Marissa were still talking, but I tried not to stare.

"Here you go, boss lady." The bartender slid me my drink. Taking a sip of the concoction, I felt my pressure rising because it was missing something.

"This isn't what I drink. What do I drink?" I yelled. She quickly grabbed my drink and tossed it out.

"Then you waste the liquor by tossing it out, all you had to do was add the Red Bull that was clearly missing. I swear to God y'all don't use the sense God gave y'all sometimes!" I spat.

"Bambino, what exactly are you assisting because you sho as hell not assisting me. In my office now!" I called out to him and marched to my office.

Bambino walked in, and his presence spoke volumes. It was something about him. We had grown up together and mostly went through the same things. I don't know why he stuck around, but he took my shit. He was good with numbers, and I trusted him to help me run the club and with my money.

"EB, I see you on one today," he calmly said as he took a seat.

Bambino was brown skin, and he rocked dreads that came down to his biceps. When he smiled, it made the ladies fall at his knees. That shit didn't work for me, though.

"Are you fraternizing with the employees? Going back on what I say goes?" I asked.

"EB no, but you were a little harsh. There is no one here, and the few that were are now gone. I know you don't give a fuck about Christmas, but you can't forget that others do. Let these ladies go home and be with their children." He sighed.

"They can go home, but you will compensate me for their wages. I hope that doesn't take from Ti'Miya's Christmas." I shrugged.

"You know if Marleigh were still alive, you wouldn't be acting like this, and you knew this was her favorite holiday. Don't worry about my child. She's gone be good regardless like she always has," he said before standing up and walking out.

Chapter 2
Bambino

Eboneigh never amazed me. She was the same ruthless, unbothered person, and it seemed like around the Christmas holiday, she was ten times worse. We grew up together, and I always had feelings for her, but she would never allow a nigga to get close after we lost our friend, Marleigh. I put up with Eboneigh shit because I knew she didn't have anyone.

Outside of being there for her, I had my own problems. EB didn't pay a nigga much. She was money-hungry, but the little I did get, I gave to most of the strippers here. A lot of the girls we had working at the club came with issues of their own, and after Eboneigh took her cut, some of them couldn't live off their earnings, which is why when she fired Marissa, I gave her a little something because she had four kids and Christmas was scarce for them.

The strippers made an okay amount if you were a top dancer and could afford to work as many hours as possible. With some being parents, it was hard for them.

The little money I gave them was nothing because I had a life outside of this damn club that EB didn't know about. She thought a nigga was broke, but I was far from it. If you were from the city and ever heard of a nigga name BK, that was me, Bambino Kratchit. My business was my business and wasn't something that I broadcasted for everyone to know. Only a handful of my workers knew that I was BK. Others thought it was some New York nigga down here with good dope.

As stated, my life was personal, especially with me being a single father to my five-year-old daughter Ti'Miya. She was my heart and main focus. This year had been the hardest for us because she suddenly started having issues with her kidneys and was needing a donor. Going back and forth to the doctor and making sure she stays on top of her diet and take all her medicines was hard when it came to a five-year-old kid.

Ti'Miya's mother wasn't in the picture, but she knew and loved her mother. This raising a daughter shit was no walk in the park. A nigga had to hire a nanny because I was always at the club with Eboneigh on top of running my drug business. I made it my duty never to miss important days and tuck her in every night even if I had to leave back out afterwards. We had breakfast every morning together no matter how tired I was. I give all praise to the women that have to do the parenting thing on their own. I have a newfound respect for them.

Walking out of EB's office, I headed to make rounds letting everyone know they could go home. First, I stopped by my office and grabbed the envelopes that I had made out for all the workers. I knew EB had cameras, so I had to be discreet with giving them all a Christmas bonus. Satisfied with the smiles I knew I was about to see, I made my rounds.

Walking up to the DJ booth, I signaled for Denzel to hand me the microphone then slid him his envelope.

"Keep that shit between us nigga, Merry Christmas. Pack up and go home," I told him. Tapping the microphone, I cleared my throat.

"Merry Christmas everyone, we are closing for the day so you guys can go home and be with your families. See you guys tomorrow at nine p.m.," I said and placed the microphone down.

Stepping out the booth, I slid to the corner that the girls had to pass to get to the room. It was dark, so EB couldn't see shit on the cameras. As each one walked by, I handed them an envelope.

Looking at my watch, I noticed it was time for me to leave the club. I promised baby girl we could bake cookies and watch movies until she fell asleep. Peeking my head back into EB's office, her face was buried in cash.

"I'm out, and everyone else is leaving as well."

"I need you to help me count this," she said, not even looking up from the money.

"EB, you done counted that money three times I know, if you keep getting the wrong amount, you getting rusty. That shit will be here. I'm going home and keeping my promise to my daughter by baking cookies and watching movies until it's time for me to play Santa. You can join us if you want to. You know you always welcomed."

"Me, baking cookies and watch you pretend to be a white man leaving gifts in a black man's house. I'll pass," she mumbled. All I could do was shake my head.

Walking over to her desk, I placed her so-called lost wages from the strippers on it. I knew it was more than enough.

"Merry Christmas, Eboneigh," I told her.

"Whatever, bah motherfucking humbug. Close the door on your way out!" she snapped.

I would continue to pray for that girl. No matter what happened, nothing in life could be that bad for her to be so insensitive.

Chapter 3
Eboneigh

Once Bambino left, I shook off all that holiday talk he was talking about. Satisfied with my final count of the money, I looked at the cameras and noticed everyone had left. Making my way to the front, I locked up the place and turned the lights out before heading back to my office. My stomach started to growl, so I decided I would call it a night as well. Everyone was going home to their families, and I couldn't wait to go home and do absolutely nothing.

With it being Christmas Eve, I decided to lock all the money in the safe instead of going to the bank. It was already dark out, and I wasn't about to go to the bank alone with all this money on me. Putting in my code, I opened the safe and stuffed all the cash inside. I placed the money that Bambino had left in my Birkin Bag, grabbed my green fur, and headed out.

The December cold was a beast, and the wind chill made it no better. Walking to my ride, I hit the locks and slid in. The smell of clean, new leather instantly hit me. As soon as the heat kicked in, I pulled off. I was so hungry that my stomach was touching my back.

However, I decided that I would just order some Uber Eats or something because it was just that cold. The ride home was silent, so I turned the radio on.

The sounds of Christmas music came blasting through the speakers, and I cringed at the sound. Instantly, I hit the station, placing it on my Apple playlist. Traffic was somewhat slow, which I assume was since everyone was out here going broke on this dumb ass holiday.

Turning into my condo garage, I parked in my space and headed into the building.

"Merry Christmas, Ms. Scroo!" the greeter greeted me. I shot him an evil look and continue to the elevator.

Man, I couldn't wait to lock myself in the house. Even the damn elevator was playing Christmas music. The Temptations' "Silent Night" was playing. I was about to lose my shit in the elevator because that was Marleigh's favorite Christmas song. As soon the elevator stopped on my floor, I flew off and marched down the hall. Removing my keys, I unlocked the door.

Entering my condo, I hung my coat on the hook and threw my keys on the table beside the door. I walked straight to my bedroom, where I started to remove my clothes. Sitting on the bed in nothing but my underwear, I combed through the Uber Eats app to see what I wanted to eat. I settled for some Chinese because the other places had closed early today.

After ordering my food, I headed to take me a shower. Letting the water cascade over my body, I was going over work in my head. With my top dancer quitting, I had to find somebody that would bring in the amount of money she was bringing in. The water got ice cold, causing me to jump and shriek out loud. I quickly turned the knobs trying to adjust the hot water, but the shit wasn't working. Stepping out, I grabbed my towel and wrapped it around my body, and turned the shower off.

Looking in the mirror, a somber mood washed over me while my stomach growled, I was hungry as hell. Slowly I headed to my room, threw on a pair of silk pajamas, and tied my hair up. Plopping on the bed, I grabbed the remote control and turned on the TV. The black and white static fuzz caused me to screw my face up because I knew it was nothing wrong with my TV. Clicking the remote several times, it was no use, so I tossed the remote across the room. The sound of the doorbell was music to my ears as I jumped off the bed and headed to the door.

Grabbing my food, I kicked the door shut in one swift motion, not even listening to the delivery guy. Sitting down at the island, I sat my food up and popped me open a beer. Beer was my guilty pleasure that I didn't drink in public. To me, beer wasn't a woman's drink, so I kept that to myself, not that I gave a fuck what anyone thought.

After eating in silence and drowning two beers, I was ready for bed. Walking back in my room, I went to brush my teeth before calling it a night. It was still rather early, close to nine p.m., and I felt the quicker I went to bed, the sooner Christmas would come and go.

Climbing into bed, I pulled the comforter up over me feeling like I was lying in the clouds. Turning off the light, I closed my eyes to let sleep take over me.

"What y'all doing out there?" a voice said as and the TV was on.

My eyes shot open, and I looked up at the TV on the wall. It was still black and white, but the white noise was gone. I wasn't sure where the voice came from, but I figured it was whatever was on TV that wasn't showing up. Sitting up, I remembered I threw the remote across the room, so I tossed the cover back and stomped out of bed. Walking over to the wall, I jerked the plug out the wall and jumped back in bed.

"Damn, a bitch just wants to sleep!" I yelled. Trying this thing again, I closed my eyes.

"I guess you didn't catch my voice the first time?"

My eyes shot open again, and they moved around the room. I know I wasn't tripping because no one was there. The TV popped on, and the fuzzy picture started to become clear. The clearer it became, the wider my mouth grew. I closed my eyes tightly because at this point, I was tripping.

"Maybe it was that damn Chinese food I ate," I mumbled.

"No bitch, it's me. Look at me! All these years, I've been gone, and you not happy to see me?"

"Maybe I'm really sleeping, and this shit a dream. Marleigh is dead and not coming back," I said aloud.

The doors to my bedroom flew open, and Marleigh entered dressed in a white, sheer floor-length robe. Her hair was teal and flowing in the prettiest curls. Marleigh's body has always been to die for. She looked like a little ghetto angel.

She moved towards the bed, and I scooted away.

"Eboneigh, you can run and hide, but I'm not going anywhere just yet. I miss you, best friend," she cooed.

Hearing her voice sent a wave of emotions through me. I could feel my shirt getting wet, and I was crying so hard. Slowly I pulled the cover down, and she was standing there smiling.

"Have I died or something? Why are you here?" I asked.

"You ain't dead yet, but if you keep living the way you are living, my girl, it's a wrap. Why the fuck is you so mean now?" She sighed and crossed her arms.

"Good, the one visit I get from my dead friend is to check me. You left remember, so the only thing I need to do is make money, and that's what I'm doing. Why is everyone worried about what I do and how I do it?" I snapped.

Marleigh came closer, and I scooted till I fell out of the bed on the other side. She started laughing while I rubbed my ass.

"Eboneigh, I couldn't control things. As your friend, I should tell you that you disappointed me. You became weak. Just because you have power and authority, walking around here like everyone just owes you the world, doesn't make you special. That shit doesn't make you this strong woman that you think you are. You hide behind your money. You pushed everyone away, even your own blood," Marleigh ranted.

I wasn't trying to hear this shit. Rolling my eyes, I let out a deep sigh.

"Ok, so why are you here if I disappoint you so much?" I asked.

"As I said earlier, I'm here to warn you. You need to change your ways. You need to see things from a different view, and that pain needs to be removed. Sometimes we must revisit things to see where things went wrong. You should be expecting a visit from three ghosts." She stopped and looked at her wrist at some little gadget.

"The fuck you mean three ghosts? I ain't got time for all this I'm still adjusting to me standing up here looking at you!" I spat.

"Scratch that change of plans. You will get three visits from me. I will be back at midnight, at one a.m., and two a.m. When I come back, you will be going with me so be prepared for some wild shit. You have no say in this whatsoever. Don't make me have to use my little powers either." Marleigh laughed. Her laugh lingered as she disappeared into thin air.

"What in the fuck is going on?" I sighed and got back in bed.

Chapter 4
Bambino

Before heading home, I had to tie up some loose ends with my main crew. When I pulled up on the block, I parked behind my homie Ced's car. The street was lit up with Christmas lights, and the winter air was colder than a motherfucker. Hitting the locks, I walked up the steps and used my key to let myself in. From the outside looking in, you would think this was a family home. I did have someone living here, but that was just for show and security. Nobody knew what we had going on here and I liked it that way.

In order to run a successful operation the way that I did, I had to stay quiet. You had to have people who were loyal and dedicated. Ced took orders from me and did exactly what I told him, but he also was smart and knew the game very well. I had no problem with him being my right hand.

When I walked into the house, Ced was sitting at the table packing up money. I knew he was getting ready for re-up. Every other day, I had my homegirl that worked for Molly Maid come out and do pick-ups. Strangers would think someone was coming out to clean house when really she was picking up and dropping off.

"My nigga, you ain't home with your football team yet?" I laughed. That nigga Ced had bout five kids. He kept his gal pregnant, but he was no dead beat, and he loved his kids.

"This my last count for the night, and then I'm headed home. Kesha's ass has been calling me to put up this damn dollhouse for the twins. A nigga needs to get high as hell before I handle all that. What you been up?" he asked.

"Nothing much, I was at the strip club the first part of the day until I talked EB into closing down. Her money-hungry ass doesn't care about the holidays," I sighed.

"She's something else, I don't see how you deal with her, but I guess you have your reasons."

"Yeah, I got faith in her one day. She will come around. Anyway, let me check the outgoing," I told him, and he handed me the iPad.

I combed through the Excel app he had with inventory in our coded products. When I said that nigga Ced was smart, I meant that shit. He was cold with technology, computers, and all that geek shit. He just chose fast money and the streets. After looking at everything and seeing that it was copasetic, I was satisfied.

"Did you make sure everyone got their Christmas bonus?" I asked him. I looked out for my workers, we were all close-knit and like a family.

"Yep, I did all that earlier. Go home and tend to Ti'Miya. We good over here." he laughed. Rubbing my chin, I laughed and dapped him up.

"Aite man, Merry Christmas," I told him.

"Merry Christmas, boss."

Exiting the house, I entered back out in the blistering cold and headed home. On the drive home, my mind drifted to my baby girl. She was all I had, and I wasn't sure how many more Christmases we were going to have with each other if her kidney condition got worse. My faith was strong, but sometimes I wondered why my child.

The thirty-minute drive to my house felt like it took forever. I don't know why it felt like everyone was just out and about tonight.

Pulling into the garage, I grabbed the few bags that I had in the back for my nanny and headed inside.

Creeping through the kitchen, I saw Ti'Miya and Latia sitting at the table laughing and full of joy. Latia saw me, but Ti'Miya had her back to me. Placing the bags down, I quietly tiptoed behind her and put my hands over her tiny face.

"Guess who?" I asked, disguising my voice.

"Daddyyy," she whined because she knew it was me. She pulled my hand down and faced me.

"You ready to bake cookies for Santa?" I asked, pulling off my coat.

"Everything is ready for you guys, and I'm going to get out of here," Latia said as she walked over to me.

"Wait a minute," I told her and went to retrieve the bags. Handing her the bags, she shook her head no.

"I can't accept this," she sighed.

"It's Christmas. Who doesn't like gifts? You are a godsend to Ti'Miya and me. You are practically family, so take these gifts and enjoy your Christmas," I demanded.

Latia smiled and nodded her head even though I knew she wanted to put up a fight.

Walking over to Ti'Miya, I lifted her and carried her to the sink.

"Let's get these hands washed, and then I'm about to bake the best cookies you ever had in your life." I laughed. We washed our hands, and I removed everything from the fridge that Latia had set up for us.

"Daddy, can I leave a cookie out for mommy?" Ti'Miya asked, causing me to damn near drop the mixing bowl.

"Um, Ti'Miya, you can do whatever you want. Will you be mad if she doesn't come and get it?" I asked. Seeing her face go from joyous to sad pulled at me.

Looking on the fridge, the card that Ti'Miya had made her mom for Mother's Day still sat there. I was tired of getting her hopes up, but Ti'Miya was so optimistic to only be five, and she didn't know any better.

"Well, this time, I told Santa, I just want a kidney and mommy for Christmas." She shrugged her shoulders.

I was speechless as I went back and forth with my thoughts and ways to smooth over this disappointment that Ti'Miya might be facing.

Chapter 5
Eboneigh

The shaking of my bed caused me to stir in my sleep. I had finally dozed off trying to forget my visit from Marleigh. When I opened my eyes, Marleigh was sitting on the edge of my bed as if she didn't have a care in the world.

"It's midnight, and I told you I would be back." I let out a frustrated sigh.

"Marleigh, I just went to sleep. You and your ghostly games aren't welcomed here," I said, turning back over.

"You do know I have the power to get you up out the bed and as bad as I want to, don't make me use force!" she snapped. Marleigh's voice rumbled, shaking the room. I quickly sat up, swinging my feet over the side of the bed.

"Happy now," I mumbled. With the quickness, my arm was snatched, and everything around me was moving so fast by me as if I was on a train.

"Now, I know some things to you are better left alone and not relived, but in order to get where you are going, you have to really grasp how you are going to get there." Marleigh looked at me and smiled.

"We both know our past wasn't the best, so prepare to walk through it again."

Marleigh waved her arm, and a mist of golden glitter filled the air. When the air cleared, we stood on the lawn of the house I last shared with my family before I was shipped off to foster care. Looking around at everything, the buildup of emotions inside was fighting to get out.

"Shall we go in?" Marleigh asked.

I shook my head no because I knew what was behind those doors and I wanted no parts. Marleigh held her hand out for me to grab and even though I didn't want to, I placed my hand in hers. Slowly we walked through the front door, and the house was freezing. Our breaths could be seen in the air; it was so cold.

"Eboneigh, where the fuck you at?" my mama yelled in a drunken stupor.

Looking down the hall, I watched a ten-year-old me come from the back room. The thin jacket I had on didn't do me any justice.

"Yes, mama?" I answered her. I adjusted the beanie hat, pulling it down on my ears because it was freezing in the house.

"Did you do what I asked you to do?" she spat. A chill went through my body as I thought about what it was she was talking about.

"Mama, it's Christmas Eve, and the security is tight," I whined.

My mother wanted me to get a funky shirt so that she could give her dope fiend ass man something for Christmas. Meanwhile, there was nothing under our makeshift tree. Looking at the tree by the wall, I saw it was something I made out of a plant mama had, hoping that it would bring some type of joy in the house.

"I swear you ain't good for nothing just like you dead beat ass daddy!" she screamed, causing me to shutter.

Mama had the worst drug addiction. The fact that she had a man to get high with, there was no need for me. She used me to do her dirty work, so I was plotting and scheming with ways to bring money into the house. Since I was young and played a shy coy role, strangers were quick to get me money.

"Fine, I'll go," was all I could muster up, and I turned around.

I felt a tear roll down my face because I knew what was about to happen next. I looked at Marleigh, and she squeezed my hand right on cue as the door was kicked in. Two mask men came barging in the house, guns aimed. I couldn't move. I was frozen in fear. Mama tried to take off running, and one grabbed her by her hair and threw her back on the couch.

"Where the fuck you think you going? Bitch, you think I don't know you stole from me. That bird ass nigga snitched on you before I blew his head off!" the man spat.

"I don't know what you talking about?" Mama yelled.

"Enough talking, Merry Christmas bitch!" the man seethed as he let out a shot hitting mama in the forehead. She flew back on the couch as blood splattered everywhere. I felt a warm liquid run down my leg because I had just pissed myself at the sight of it all.

"Let's go, nigga!" the other man yelled.

The one that shot my mama walked over to me and lifted his gun to my head. At that moment I was scared, but I didn't cry. I looked down the barrel of the gun and said a silent prayer. He lowered his weapon and bent down towards me. His eyes were coal black.

"You a shooter, you just don't know it yet. I saved your life by sparing you from these misfits that were raising you." He laughed.

The man reached into his pocket and pulled out a wad of cash, sticking in my pissy pants pocket. No other words were spoken, and he and the man were out that fast.

"Marleigh, I don't want to see no more of this shit!" I spat and turned to walk away. I sho as hell didn't want to see my dead ass mammy.

"We may be done here, but we're not done, EB." She sighed and waved her arm across my face.

I starting coughing at all the glitter I was already over this shit. This was about to be the longest night in history.

Chapter 6
Eboneigh

"I'm sorry you had to see that again," Marleigh apologized as we traveled to the next place. All I did was shake my head. I was numb to it and buried it in the back of my head.

"It's all good, Marleigh. I guess that's what you set out to do." I sighed.

"Quit being a bitch. This is the reason why you're here now. Let that pain up out you and learn from that shit!" she spat.

When the glitter cleared, we were at The Santana's. The Santana's were the foster family that took me in after the death of my mom. Following her death, I bounced around for an entire year until The Santana's had room for me. I moved in a week before Christmas when I was twelve. Marleigh led us through the door, and there stood a twelve-year-old me standing in front of Mr. and Mrs. Santana with my small trash bag of belongings.

"We are so glad to have you in our home," Mrs. Santana cooed.

Marleigh and I both started laughing because her fraud ass was a joke.

"Marleigh, come show Eboneigh to you guys room!" she yelled out, and twelve-year-old Marleigh came marching down the stairs.

Seeing another girl my age made me feel better, but I was also skeptical because the girls I had come across in the system were ruthless to newbies. Marleigh waved at me, and I shot her a half smile.

"Come on," Marleigh told me. I followed her upstairs. Marleigh and I followed our younger selves up the stairs and to our old bedroom that we shared.

"You can have that bed," Marleigh told me, and I placed the trash bag on the bed and started to unpack my things.

I was a neat freak wherever I went because this was all I had. The Santana's had the room set up nice with twin beds and dressers on both sides. Turning to Marleigh, she just kept looking at me.

"I almost whooped your ass that day for staring so hard," I joked, looking at Marleigh.

"Girl, you wish. I was staring at you because all I saw was another lost girl thinking she found the perfect foster family when truthfully, you didn't know what was heading your way." Marleigh sighed.

That day when I moved with the Santana's, Marleigh and I created a bond like no other. We became each other's protectors. We both turned back around and focused back on ourselves.

"How long have you been here?" I asked Marleigh.

"Six months."

"Are they good people? This house is amazing."

I looked around the room. I don't know what they did for a living, but this probably was the best foster house I ever stayed in. The space was huge, and the house was decked out. Didn't give you the impression that kids lived here.

Marleigh made her way over to the bed and sat next to me.

"Mrs. Santana is sweet as pie because she does everything around here and sees nothing. It's her husband who is a fucking bitch. He takes all the checks and pocket the money. I literally have to steal when I need things like personal items and even clothes. Whatever you come here with, that's about all you leave with. It's a fucking shame. They just put on a big ass front for their friends and the nosey ass neighbors." Marleigh shook her head. Here I was thinking I had stepped in a better environment, only to learn I was still fucked.

"I make the best of it, though, because I could be somewhere far worse. One family I stayed with, the daddy couldn't keep his hands to himself at night." Marleigh shrugged her shoulders. I could tell she was a strong girl.

"Well, I got your back here if you promise to have mine?" I told her because, at this point, I had nobody else.

"I can do that." Marleigh smiled.

She jumped out of bed and ran over to the window. Turning around, she motioned for me to come over, so I eased off the bed and ran to her side. Looking out the window, she smiled at some boy that was out there.

"Let's go. I have to introduce you to the Bam." She giggled. Marleigh grabbed my hand as we ran down the steps.

I looked at Marleigh, and she shook her head at me, waving her arm sending us outside, getting there before the younger us made it outside. Seeing Bambino at his young age when we first met actually put a smile on my face. Here we all were again. Marleigh, Bambino, and I were one.

"You were in love with that boy, still is, but I ain't gone tell nobody. Y'all were supposed to get married." Marleigh laughed.

"Bitch, fuck you. It was never like that for us." I rolled my eyes and tuned in on the conversation.

"Wassup Marleigh, y'all got a new victim in the house?" Bam looked at me and winked his eyes. He was a sight to see. I knew I was blushing like hell.

"This is Eboneigh, and yeah, she's new to the house. Eboneigh, this is Bambino," she said, introducing us.

"Wassup EB, you cute and shit." I could see Bambino had no filter.

"Thank you," was all I said.

The rest of the day, we hung out with Bambino, and as I got to know him, things between us did bring us a little closer. Marleigh looked at me and waved her arm, sending us to Christmas morning at The Santana's.

"EB, wake up!" Marleigh shook me from my slumber. Opening my eyes, I wanted to roll back over and go to sleep.

"What Marleigh, what time is it?" I mumbled.

"Does it matter? It's Christmas!" she shouted.

I was still in a little funk last night was hard for me to get some sleep due to it being my mom's death anniversary.

"Look," Marleigh demanded, pointing to the corner in our room. When I looked up, there was a tiny table tree in the corner that had some lights on it. It wasn't there the night before.

I looked over at my angel Marleigh because I remember this day like it happened yesterday. I almost forgot how happy I was that day. Marleigh looked at me.

"How could you bury this memory after all these years?" she whispered and shook her head. Turning back, I tried to keep the tears from falling from feeling like shit.

"Where did that come from?" I asked, lifting and removing the covers.

"It sho ain't from the Santana's. Most of these have your name on them. Come on, open them up!" she gassed me up.

I couldn't understand why she was so excited because, from the looks of it, she didn't have anything underneath the tree. Slowly I started opening the boxes, and they were filled with clothing, underclothes, bras, toiletries. It was all the small stuff that I needed because I was growing out of the shit I came with. I continued to open the boxes, and there was a coat as well. I even had a nice pair of boots.

"Here, this one is from me." Marleigh smiled, shoving the small box in my hand.

I turned away from the scene because I didn't want to see anymore. Grabbing my necklace that was around my neck, I closed my eyes. I felt like I was about to pass out.

"You need to see this EB, turn around," Marleigh's voice echoed in my ears.

I got control of my breathing and slowly turned back around to face the scene, watching Marleigh stand over me, waiting on me to open the box. I watched as I opened the box and traced my finger over a piece of a golden heart necklace.

"Marleigh, where did you get this?" I asked because I wasn't sure if she stole it or not. She was good at that.

"Read it." She smiled.

"Sister's Forever M & E," I read aloud.

"You didn't have to get me all of this stuff," I complained.

"Oh, I didn't get you all that other stuff. I only got you the necklace. Bambino got you all that stuff. That boy really likes you, and he has a good heart," Marleigh smiled.

The room fell silent, and Marleigh looked at me, still holding the necklace around my neck. She wore a frown of disappointment.

"Eboneigh, it's clear you never take that necklace off. After my death, how could you turn so cold and I've always been near your heart and in it?" she asked me.

"I don't know, Marleigh," I admitted.

Marleigh grabbed my hand, and we left fast as hell.

Chapter 7
Eboneigh

When we stopped, I rolled my eyes as we landed in the living room of our two-bedroom duplex — man, how I remember this raggedy ass place. Marleigh and I were nineteen, and Bambino was twenty-one now. We end up staying with the Santana's up until we turned eighteen, and we left together. I always used to tell her how it was all God that he allowed us to grow up together and not be separated. I can't emphasize how much Marleigh and even Bambino was all the family I had.

Bambino lived at the duplex with us. Marleigh and I continued to share a room, and he had his own room to give him privacy. Thanks to him and his little corner hustling and serving the landlord, he looked out for us by letting us rent out his place. This is where our lives took a turn. Things became fast-paced, and we were out here in these streets wild.

"I remember nights. I didn't remember nights!" Marleigh smiled, quoting Jeezy.

"Man yeah, we had some cool lit times here," I admitted.

The door flew opened, and Marleigh and I stood off to the side, watching the scene take place. Bambino came barging in the house and headed straight to our room. Marleigh was gone, and I was lying across the bed, coming down off a weed induced high. The door to my bedroom came flying open, and Bambino stood there like he wanted to kill me.

"What the fuck you coming in here like that for?" I asked, jumping damn near out my skin.

"Why am I'm hearing that you down there working with Marleigh at the strip club?" he spat.

"He always did try to be somebody daddy?" I mumbled to Marleigh.

"EB, you ain't that damn blind. Bam just didn't want the woman he loved shaking her ass." Marleigh laughed, doing a little twerk. I waved her off and focused back on the scene.

"First of all, you don't have any say on what I do. Marleigh makes a decent amount of money and with us both bringing in that cash, it will help you out. This little penny-any shit you doing is barely taking care of us. Selling drugs ain't your thing, Bam," I told him.

One thing I peeped about Bambino was he always was a hustler, but he was smart. That nigga could build a computer and work numbers with his eyes closed. This street shit wasn't for him.

"So what I do ain't good enough around here? Have you ever wanted for anything? Do you ever go hungry? Don't you always have water to wash your ass, Eboneigh? Why all of a sudden you so money hungry?" he spat.

"At this point, I don't even know why we still watching this because we all know how Bambino turned out — working for me as usual. I sign his checks, so now who's taking care of who?" I spat.

"Yet, you end up having—"

"Shut the fuck up, Marleigh," I cut her off because I knew what she was about to let fly out of her mouth.

"Yeah, I may not be here physically, but I know everything that takes place in your life. Turn around and listen good!" Marleigh spat.

She's lucky I couldn't fight a ghost because I wanted to go in her shit.

"It's not about being money-hungry, Bam. If we can use the extra cash, I don't see a problem. As soon as you get in your head that you and I are not an item. There will never be a you and me. We fuck from time to time, and that's all. Please keep your feelings in check, and don't let it ruin our friendship," I told him.

"That was pretty harsh," Marleigh mumbled.

"Are you going to have commentary for every stop because I'm tired of your mouth and honestly tired of this whole damn revisit the past shit? All this shit is irrelevant," I seethed.

Marleigh didn't even answer. She just pointed at the scene. Turning around Bambino was walking out of the bedroom, and he didn't utter a word after the whiplash I gave him.

"One day you gone see that I will be that nigga in these streets. No matter what, I will always be by your side," Bambino mumbled and walked to his bedroom.

"Oh my god, are we done? He ain't said shit important!" I yelled out in aggravation. Inside I was hurting because one thing did stick out. He was still by my side. I never said Bambino was a bad guy. He has a heart of gold. It just wasn't for me.

Marleigh shook her head in disappointment and waved her arms, sending us on another glitter induced ride through the sky. I was done talking to Marleigh, and I wanted to be back home in my bed.

When we stopped, I realized we were at our old stomping grounds. Tootie B's was the place to be. We stood off to the side and watched the crowd. Looking up on stage, Marleigh was doing her set. I let out a frustrated sigh because I remembered this night. Looking towards the stage, I saw myself cheering her own while waiting to do my set when she finished up. Marleigh knew how to work a damn pole. She was the coldest at the shit. I paid attention to the guy in the front that kept throwing money up on stage, and she was eating it up.

We had our regulars in the club, and some tipped more than others. When Marleigh scooted back from the mystery man, one of her regulars begin to throw money her way, so she focused her attention on him trying to make his money, of course.

My eyes stayed on the guy that she was dancing with at first because he didn't like that shit. He stood up and made his way to the side of the stage keeping his eyes on Marleigh. When Marleigh saw him, she stopped dancing and exited the stage fast as hell.

I started to follow, but then my name was called.

"EB, skip the next set and head to the private room. Someone has requested you, and the pay is well. I must say you might have an admirer," my boss demanded. Looking back over my shoulder. I assumed Marleigh was alright because the guy was walking back out and headed towards the exit. Shrugging my shoulders, I headed upstairs to the private lounges.

When I entered the room, Bambino was sitting on the couch.

"Bam, what the hell are you doing here? Please don't start this playing shit on my job. I was about to go on stage!" I spat. He was taking this shit too far.

"I was just paying for a dance. Then you can do whatever it is you do." He shrugged.

"You still don't see how much he loves you?" Marleigh whispered.

"He did do that shit for a week straight, didn't he?"

I laughed because I swear after that night. That man made sure he paid me for a private dance every single night. I don't know where he was getting the money from, but he didn't even try to short me.

"Do we have to watch what happened this night because I already know what happened?" I asked Marleigh.

"No, I want to watch. We don't have porn up there." Marleigh pointed to the sky.

"Marleigh, let's go," I demanded, and she started pouting like a damn little kid. We ended up back downstairs and in the dressing room.

Marleigh's head laid on her vanity, and I walked up behind her.

"Yo, what the fuck was up with that nigga?" I asked her. When Marleigh lifted her head, her eye was swollen shut.

"Did he do this to you?" I yelled. Marleigh started to stand up and grab me by my arms.

"It's ok. I hit him first. He was just upset, calm down."

I looked over at Marleigh, and she was crying. How could she even re-watch this part of my life? Had she left, then she would still be alive.

"I know what you're thinking EB, and we are here for you not me. What's done is done."

Marleigh sighed and waved her arm. I didn't want to go to another scene. I didn't want to see anything else from my past because I knew what was coming next.

"Marleigh, can we please just go? I can't do this anymore," I cried. The tears were falling, and they wouldn't stop.

"It's ok, EB. I promise you I'll be right there with you," was all she said, and we continued on our journey to the next stop.

It was Christmas Eve, and I had just made my way back from the grocery store. Marleigh was sitting in the living room, wrapping some things we had gotten for Bam for Christmas.

"Girl, next year, we will go shopping way before Christmas because that crowd out there was disrespectful. It's so many folks out there, and shit's been picked over." I sighed, placing the groceries in the kitchen.

Once I put the groceries up, I grabbed two mugs from the cabinet and started to make Marleigh and me some hot chocolate. Over the years, we had created our own tradition that we shared in our bedroom at the Santana's up until we moved out.

Marleigh loved Christmas, and even though Christmas Eve was a bad day for me and harbored terrible memories, she pulled me up out of that funk by creating new ones. When the hot chocolate was done, I grabbed the tin of Christmas cookies that we always ate and headed into the living room.

"I know it's still early, but since you won't be here tonight, I figured we still do our tradition until it's time for you to leave." I smiled, handing her a mug.

"I see you put extra marshmallows in there like I like." She smiled. Marleigh placed *A Diva's Christmas Carol* in the DVD player and started the movie. I pulled the blanket over our legs, and we sipped our hot chocolate and ate cookies.

"Good times." I smiled at Marleigh, and she winked at me. That was something that I rarely did, but she got one out of me because I missed our times together.

We both turned towards the door when we heard the keys jiggling, and Bambino walked in taking off his coat.

"Aw shit, I'm just in time," he said, and he climbed on the couch between the both of us.

"Don't you have better things to do?" I asked him.

"Nope, something told me to come home and chill with y'all, so I did. Is that a problem, EB?" he asked. I rolled my eyes at him and focused back on the movie.

Marleigh's phone kept going off during the movie, and she would just look at it and place it back down. Me standing here watching this all take place again and breaking it down, there were so many signs. Who would have ever thought this was our last night together as a family? It was something in me that wanted to spend that time with my girl like I knew deep down inside it was our last. Then Bambino coming home and saying that something told him to come home. God was preparing us. I wish I had opened my mouth and asked Marleigh who was blowing up her phone, and I wish I would've convince her to stay that night instead of going with her boyfriend.

I never liked him from the very first time he put his hands on her. I used to ask myself all the time why in the hell did she accept that from him because she wasn't the type of female that took anything from a nigga. Marleigh was strong-willed and most guys had issues with dating her because she didn't play about her money, and she liked to be in control of things.

When the movie was over, we cleaned up our mess, and Marleigh started to get ready. My mood was down, so Bambino offered to stay in with me, and I let him. Bambino sat on the other end of the couch, and he was in his phone. I just watched him. He was in the stage of growing his dreads, but they looked nice. He kept his face trimmed, not to mention his smile. I assumed he felt me looking at him because he looked up and we locked eyes.

"Aw hell, what I do now?" he asked.

"Nothing, boy, I was just looking at your ugly ass," I lied. Marleigh came out of the room carrying her bag.

"I'll be back first thing in the morning, so don't open the gifts without me," she demanded.

"Aite girl," I waved her off. She winked at Bambino, and I caught that shit, then she walked out the door.

As soon as the door closed, Bambino made his way in between my legs. Ok yeah, I acted like I hated his guts, but his sex game was off the chain, and I wasn't about to turn down no head or no dick down. I slid out of my pants and opened my legs for him. My body would submit to him, and I could feel the heat in between my legs.

While he placed his tongue in my center, I closed my eyes and let the feeling run through me. Bam was my first and only. I'd been fucking him since the Santana's. I just grew accustomed to him, and even though I would talk to guys, I didn't sexually want them.

Bambino took his time, and the lights from the Christmas tree had the room lit perfectly. Using my hands, I rubbed them through his hair as I grind into his face.

"Ok yeah, I think it's time to stop," I said because I was getting turned on watching Bambino and I carry on.

"Party pooper." Marleigh sighed and waved her hand.

The ringing of my cell phone woke me up out of my slumber. Bam and I had fallen asleep on the couch after our session, and I couldn't believe I was lying in his arms. The phone rang again, and I leaned over and grabbed it off the table. Seeing that it was Marleigh, I answered the phone.

"Hello," I answered groggily.

"EB, please come and get me, he is going to kill me!" she cried into the phone. I pushed Bambino and sat up on the couch.

"Where are you? I knew you should've stayed your ass at home!" I spat.

"2229 Bosier… Ahhhhh!" Marleigh could be heard screaming, and the call ended. I jumped off the couch and started to put my clothes on in a panic.

"What the fuck is going on?" Bambino asked.

"That was Marleigh. She was talking about he was going to kill her," I had no time to think.

"What the fuck is going on?" he said, scrambling to get his clothes as well.

"We never told you this, but that nigga be putting his hands on Marleigh. She said he had stopped, but if you would've heard her voice on that phone. We need to call the police!" I screamed.

"She started to tell me the address, then the call dropped. This can't be happening."

I panicked as I dialed 9-1-1 and told them what was happening. They were able to find the address off of what I had given them. Bambino and I left the house and headed to the address as well. Marleigh was twenty minutes away, and the drive felt like forever. During the entire trip, I prayed like hell that my girl was ok.

When I looked over at Marleigh, she was crying. I reached over and placed my hand in hers. Like she told me, she was going to be here through this with me, so it was only right that I be here for her as we endured this together. I placed my head on her shoulders as we watched as Bambino and I pull up outside to an ambulance and police cars everywhere. We both hopped out of the car and ran towards the crime scene tape and was stopped by a uniform officer.

"You can't go in there. This is a crime scene," he said, holding his hand up.

"I'm the one that called the police. Can you please tell me my friend is ok?" I asked.

"Ma'am if you calm down. I will get that information for you," he said, but I tuned him out when I looked over his shoulder and seen them wheeling out someone on the stretcher in a black bag. My eyes diverted to the cops behind them, and when I noticed that bitch ass nigga walk out in handcuffs, I ran to the stretcher.

"Please, this is my foster sister and next to kin. I was the one that placed the call to send police here because she called me saying he was going to kill her. I need to see her. I need to know if that is my sister in that bag," I cried.

The medical people looked at the detective, and he nodded his head. They sat the stretcher down and unzipped the bag. Vomit went flying when I saw Marleigh's face. I was hysterical and couldn't control my emotions.

"Marleigh, nooooo! Why did you leave me? I was coming baby!" I cried. Bambino had tears streaming down his face as he held me on the ground.

"That bitch ass nigga killed my sister!" I spat.

When he was placed in the back of the car, I locked eyes with him and vowed never to forget a motherfucking face.

"Marleigh enough, please take me back home!" I pleaded. This time she nodded her head and then waved her arm.

Chapter 8
Eboneigh

I was back in my bedroom once the glitter cleared, and I had never been happier to see home, enduring all that shit made my head hurt. There were nothing but tragedies.

"You might as well not even bother going to sleep because I will be back in the next hour. I know some things were hard to watch, but I hope you took something from at least some of it, mainly those that care about you and those that would hate to see you the way that you are. It's okay to grieve, but I'm fine EB, and the life you're living is miserable. We struggled, but it made us who we are. I loved you like a real sister, and whether or not you see it, Bam loves you too and always has.

When I left you that money making you my beneficiary, I wanted you to succeed, which you have, but at what cost? When I come back, you will get a chance to see the lives that you have affected just by being you." Marleigh smiled.

All I could do was nod my head, and I flopped back on the bed. Letting out a deep sigh, I closed my eyes and attempted to let sleep take over.

***

The loud ringing of a bell woke me from my slumber. Pouting like a little child, I kicked my feet in the air and sat up. Marleigh sat in the corner with her head rested upon her hand and legs crossed.

"I guess you comfortable, huh?" I asked Marleigh. Marleigh uncrossed her legs and shrugged her shoulders.

"It's good to sit down, considering all the runs we made and are about to make. I hope that you let your brain rest because this may get harder and harder for you," Marleigh voiced.

"I'm ready. Can we go so we can get this over with?" I sighed. Marleigh shrugged her shoulders and stood up. I followed her through the hallway of my condo, and we took a seat on the couch.

"So, what we are watching this go-round on the TV?" I asked.

"Just hush and sit down," Marleigh demanded.

Doing as I was told, I took a seat on the couch beside her. Marleigh smiled then snapped her fingers. The couch zoomed through the wall, and we were flying over the city.

"I swear they shouldn't have given you no type of powers. You are so over the top." I chuckled.

We came to an abrupt stop, and the area was extremely nice. I knew about this area but opted to move closer to the club.

"Who the hell lives out here?" I asked.

Marleigh didn't say anything. She pointed to a car coming up the street, and I knew who car it was — Marissa. I turned my nose up.

"I know this can't be her home. Just how much am I paying her ass?" I said through gritted teeth. I watched as Marissa got out the car with her work bag, displaying a look of disappointment on her face.

"You and Marissa seem to bump heads a lot. She strong-minded like you, huh?" Marleigh asked.

"She's disrespectful that's all that is!" I snapped.

"EB, everyone is not going to let you talk to them any kind of way. You might place fear in most the people you cross, but you got some that won't tolerate it, and she seems to be your medicine," Marleigh laughed. She reached out for my arm, and we headed into Marissa's house.

When we entered the house, it was bare. The living room furniture, which consisted of two couches, was all that was there. A Charlie Brown Christmas tree sat in the corner.

"I'm home!" she called out and three kids came running around the corner.

"Mommy!" they yelled.

I knew she had kids, but not three of them motherfuckers. Then another kid came around the corner, making four and he looked to be about sixteen.

"Did you make the money?" he asked.

Marissa gave him a somber look then held her head down. She stood up and ran her fingers through her hair.

"Y'all come over here and sit down let me talk to you guys for a minute," she told the children.

They all lined up on the bigger couch while the older one stood off to the side. He had an attitude just like her.

"I know I told you guys that if I worked today, I would be able to get you guys' one thing for Christmas. My boss and I had some words, and I lost my job. Now BK did give me some money, but I had to think rationally and went ahead and paid the rent for next month," she sighed.

"Man, why the hell you move us all the way out here anyway and we got to suffer for that shit?" the older boy spat.

"Oh, he needs he his ass beat," I whispered to Marleigh.

"Darius, excuse me for wanting to give y'all something I never had. I want you all to be bigger and greater than me. Look at me, how do you feel about your mother being a stripper? I have no education or qualifications so that I can get a decent job. This is our home. We may not have much in here, but you come home to a beautiful house that is yours. Every penny I make goes to this house and to get you guys the best education. I will dance until my feet bleed so that y'all could at least get that. Coming up, I had to bathe with water bottles because the water was cut off for days at a time. That's why I'm always paying all the bills first and make sure y'all have a hot meal. All that other shit is materialistic. Did you forget about Mee-Maw back there, and I'm responsible for her medicine and needs," Marissa cried.

"EB, just how much are you taking out of these girls' earnings to where she can't even get her kids a decent Christmas," Marleigh shook her head.

"On a good night, she probably takes home at least four or five hundred." I shrugged.

"You have got to be kidding me. EB, that's probably one of these kids' tuition for a month."

"Well, it's not my fault that she got all these kids. She shouldn't try to live above her means." I shrugged. Marleigh rolled her eyes.

"I'm sorry for being harsh, mama. I guess I never looked at it like that, but don't cry," Darius said and walked over to hug his mama.

"Christmas is about love and family anyway. So, we will have a good one, regardless. I'm going to cook a nice meal, and I don't have to work so I'll be here all day. Hopefully, I can get on somewhere else, and I will try to get you guys something after Christmas," Marissa told her son.

"Can you get them situated while I go check on Mee-Maw?" she told him.

Marissa headed off to the back, and we followed as she wiped the tears that were streaming down her face. When we entered a room, an older lady laid in a hospital bed, and she didn't look so good. Marissa walked over to the bed and checked her medicine tray.

"Mee-Maw, I'm home," she said in a low tone.

The lady shifted her head, and she slowly lifted her finger. Marissa kneeled close to her, and she rubbed the side of Marissa's face with her finger, half smiling.

"You happy to see me?" she asked the woman. She rubbed her face again and nodded her head.

"I'll be here more now for a little while. I have to make a call, and I'll be back to give you your medicine. I got to get these kids Christmas somehow," she told the old lady. Marissa walked away from the bed.

We walked towards the door as she stepped out in the hall and retrieved her phone.

"I really hate to call BK after he just gave me some money, but I just want my kids to be happy," she said aloud.

"Who is this BK nigga she keeps speaking on?" I turned to ask Marleigh. Marleigh shrugged her shoulders. I felt she was lying.

Marissa placed the call, and she walked into her bedroom and closed the door. We could hear the phone ringing because she had it on speaker.

"Sup, Marissa!" his voice boomed through the phone. My mouth dropped because I knew that fucking voice. I looked at Marleigh, and a smirk graced her face.

"Hey BK,"

"Don't call me that. I'm at home," he interrupted her.

"I'm sorry, Bambino," she mumbled.

"I knew he was fucking her nasty ass!" I shouted as if anyone could hear me beside Marleigh.

"Are you mad? You made it clear that you didn't want him, right?" Marleigh asked.

I don't know why, but I felt a way that she was calling Bam and why the fuck was he called BK.

"Look, I really appreciate you coming through for me today after EB fired me. You sort of know my situation, and I hate to do this, but since EB fired me, I had no choice but to pay my rent with the money you gave because I might not have the money to pay it next month if I don't find something soon. My kids were so disappointed because I promised them if I worked today, I would get them all at least one thing for Christmas."

"You need some more money, Marissa?" Bam just flat out asked.

"Yes, not much, I just want them to wake up to something," she cried.

"Don't start all that crying, I'll Cash App you some cash, and you go take care of that. Merry Christmas," was all he said and ended the call.

Marissa dropped the phone and placed her hands together as if she was praying to the gods.

"Thank you, Lord," she cried.

The Cash App sound dinged on her phone, and she quickly picked it up. Her eyes widened, and I moved closer to see what exactly he sent her. My eyes bucked. This nigga sent her five grand.

"If she ain't popping pussy, then I don't know what she's doing. Bam just sent her five thousand dollars and where the hell did he get this type of cash. Let me find out this nigga stealing from me!" I snapped.

Marissa grabbed her things and headed back out to the front.

"Mommy will be back. I have to make a few runs. Be on your best behavior. Otherwise, Santa won't come see you younger ones," she told the kids with a smile on her face.

Marleigh waved her hands, and we end up at Wal-Mart, where Marissa grabbed all four of her kids' one item that they really wanted and a few clothes. I figured she would spend all the money, but instead, she grabbed a few money orders as well for tuition. It was good to see that she didn't blow the money, but my beef was with

Bam, BK, or whoever the fuck he called himself these days. All these thoughts went through my head because I prayed to God that he wouldn't do something so low as to steal from me.

"Girl, it's time you get some answers before you have a stroke and be up here with me." Marleigh laughed. I didn't see that shit funny.

Marleigh snapped her finger, and we stood across the street in some neighborhood, not knowing where we were at.

"Now, who the hell lives here?" I asked.

Marleigh pointed as Bambino's truck rolled up and parked in the driveway. I knew this wasn't his house so what was he doing here. I watched as he pulled his coat closed and walked the steps to enter the house. Marleigh signaled for me to come on, and I followed closely behind her. When we stepped into the house, Bam was already in a conversation with Ced. I had met him a few times before.

When I heard Bam ask him about some money and re-upping and shit, I put two and two together. I know he ain't doing what I think he's doing? The amount that Ced counted was huge, and I could eyeball that shit and tell it because I knew my money.

"This nigga way too smart to get his hands dirty. I can't believe he resorted back to the streets," I told Marleigh.

"That's the things Bam is brilliant, and he's able to run a successful operation without actually getting his hands dirty. That man has never left your side. You pay him the bare minimum to help you with your business. You threw around the fact that you had given him a job, but it looks to be that he might be working with you just to have you in his presence. I don't see how he do it? Bam has some hope in you that you don't even see in yourself. You guys' situation is bigger than this, though, and you know it," Marleigh told me.

Bam was BK out here pushing weight and making big bucks. I remember telling him the streets wasn't for him, but look what he did for himself, and he did it discreetly. This man was out here making more money than me, which explains the free cash that he was giving out to Marissa and shit. I fixed my eyes back on Bambino as he scanned an iPad and just looked to be making boss moves. He asked Ced about the Christmas bonuses for his workers and made sure everyone was straight. That was Bambino all the way around. He was loyal and loving to those that were the same to him.

"Ok, now that you showed me Bam was a kingpin, can we go?" I asked Marleigh.

"Why you in such a hurry? You don't want to face what you know is coming next?" Marleigh snapped.

I waved her off because she was speaking the truth. We watched Bam as he left the house, and we walked down the steps, and I prepared to be shipped off to a place I didn't want to go. Marleigh snapped her little ass fingers, and we stood in the home of Bambino.

Chapter 9
Eboneigh

When we came to our stop, I was expecting to be standing in Bambino's apartment because that was what I thought was his home. This place we were in was different, and I had never been here before. This man was really holding out on me. It was like he was full of secrets, and I didn't know who he was anymore.

Bambino entered the house, and he snuck in. Ti'Miya was sitting at the table with her nanny. Watching him interact with her made me smile. That girl loved her daddy, and it was apparent how she reacted when he came into the room. Bam always had a beautiful smile, but it was different around his daughter.

I watched as he gave her nanny a few gift bags and sent her on her way. I walked closer to him and Ti'Miya while they were in the kitchen about to make cookies. Walking over to the fridge, it was filled with artwork, and my eyes landed on a Mother's Day card. Glancing over it, I turned my head at Ti'Miya and Bam as they gathered the things to bake cookies.

"Daddy, can I leave a cookie out for Mommy?" Ti'Miya asked Bam. Bam hesitated with his answer as if it hurt him to answer her.

"It's a damn shame. Ti'Miya's mama ain't shit!" Marleigh spat.

"I agree," I mumbled.

Just watching them together, my emotions were all over the place, and my heartstrings were being played like a guitar. When they finished baking cookies, I followed them to the living room, where I took a seat on the couch beside them. Bambino started a movie for them to watch and I laughed at the selection.

"Would you look at this?" I told Marleigh. Bambino had her watching *A Diva's Christmas Carol.*

"Traditions were made to be followed, at least someone remembered." Marleigh sighed.

I don't know what was wrong with her this go-round, but Marleigh was being real bitchy.

"Daddy, she's mean," Ti'Miya spoke out, referring to the main character in the movie.

"She's not mean baby, just misunderstood," he replied.

"Daddy," Ti'Miya whispered. Bam looked down at her and rubbed her head.

"Yes, baby girl?"

"Will I get a new body part or die?" she asked, and my face frowned up because I wasn't sure what she was talking about.

"Hopefully, you can get it so that you won't be sick anymore. You let daddy worry about that, and you just worry about Santa," he smiled.

I stood up from the couch and walked over to Bambino's face, searching his face because it was etched in fear. It was like he felt me there, but I knew he couldn't see me. Turning to Marleigh, I needed answers.

"What's going on with Ti'Miya since you seem to know everything?" I snapped. Marleigh crossed her arms and flipped her hair.

"I'm not the one you should be mad at. Why do I know everything, and you don't is the question?" Marleigh snapped back at me. I closed my eyes and let out a deep breath.

"Please tell me what's going on with her?" I pleaded.

Marleigh snapped her fingers, and we ended up in the doctor's office. Bambino sat with his head in his hands as the doctor looked over all the papers that were sitting in front of him.

"Mr. Kratchit, after looking over everything, the issues with Ti'Miya is resulting in bad kidney function. She needs a kidney because hers is failing. Now, I have the number for a dietitian here that I need you to visit because while we wait on a kidney donor. She will need to be on a strict diet and take these medicines so that the damage to the bad kidney won't progress."

Bambino had tears in his eyes at the news that the doctor had given him. He looks like he had the weight of the world on his shoulders. How could he keep something like this a secret? It's no telling all the stress he had on him due to this.

"Well, since I'm her father, I can be a donor, right?" he quickly asked.

"That's true. We just need to run a few tests to make sure you are fully compatible. I know that you are doing this alone, and I commend you, but if you don't match, you may need to reach out to her mother. With being placed on a donor list, there's no telling how long Ti'Miya may need to wait. So the sooner, the better," the doctor informed him.

I bit down at my bottom lip while listening to Bambino and the doctor's conversation.

"I take it that Bam wasn't a match since they still waiting for a donor?" I asked Marleigh. All she did was nod her head.

I walked out of the room and had no clue where I was going, but I no longer wanted to listen to them. As soon as I walked out the door, I was back at Bambino's crib, and he had just placed Ti'Miya in the bed. My heart broke looking at her. Bam tucked her in and turned her night light on before heading to his own room. Once inside, he sat on his bed and removed a note from his bedside drawer.

Being me, I had to see what it said, so I walked over and took a seat beside him. For some reason, when I sat down, he looked at me, and it freaked me out.

"He can't see you, but he can feel a presence," Marleigh told me.

He placed his focus back on the letter that he held in his hand. I skimmed over the letter, and a drop of water hit the paper. Bam was crying. I haven't seen him cry since Marleigh's funeral.

"This shit ain't fair, bruh!" he said to nobody, but I assume he was talking to God.

Looking back at the letter, it was a Christmas list that Ti'Miya wrote. In an instant, he balled the letter up and threw it at the wall.

"Out of everything that money can buy, my child asks me for something that I can't give her. What am I to tell her when she sees Santa ain't bring her no kidney or her mama? That's all she wants, and I failed!" he spat, punching his hand.

"God, you know I'm constantly praying for a change in my situation. I don't know what else to do. I try to keep going for the sake of my child, but Lord knows I don't know how much more I can take. If you hear me, help me out on this." Bam grabbed the bridge of his nose and let out a deep sigh.

"Amen," he said and stood up to remove his shirt.

I continued to sit on the bed because I was frozen as he headed to take a shower. I was numb and had seen enough. Walking over to Marleigh, she looked like a mother of a child that was fed up. She waved both her arms in the air, and we disappeared.

Once the dust settled, I was back in my bedroom. Pacing the floor, I was trying to get my thoughts together.

"Look, I don't have much to say, but I do know I have to say whatever it is before the third visit. Eboneigh, I love you so much. It hurts to see this person that you turned in to. If anyone knows your pain from growing up, you know I do. I've always looked out for you and tried to make sure you were good, even after my death. There are so many people hurting because of you, and all that can be fixed if you right your wrongs. Just because you lost your mother, me, and whatever else that damaged you, doesn't mean you shut everyone out. You should want a family more than anything because that was the route we were taking before I had to leave. If you don't do it for yourself, do it for the ones that love you and me. Love them back. You get more blessings when you bless others. Just know that even though

I might not be here physically, I have never left your side, and I don't plan on it even in the afterlife." Marleigh smiled.

Marleigh placed her hands on both sides of my face.

"I love you, sister," she cried. As soon as she cried, I did the same.

"I love you more," I told her and fell into her arms.

I hugged her and didn't let her go. It felt good to be her arms. When I looked in the mirror, all I saw was my reflection and my arms holding nothing but air. Sleep was nonexistent at this point, so I took a seat in the chair I had in the corner of my room and just watched the clock.

Chapter 10
Eboneigh

After staring at the clock for a while, my eyes shifted to my bedroom door. The door was closed, but I could hear noise coming from the other side. There were loud thumps like someone was banging on the wall. The clawing at the door had me scoot back in my chair some. The next thing you know, smoke started to come from underneath the door. Panic set in because maybe somebody had come in my condo and set it on fire. So, I slowly eased off the chair and tiptoed to the door. When I reached for the handle, the door flew open, and I let out a piercing scream at what I saw.

In all black, there stood Marleigh. Her hair wasn't the same as the previous visits. It was unkempt and looked a mess. Her once flawless skin was pale in color, damn near white like Beetlejuice. The darkness of her eyes made it impossible to look at her. If I wasn't creeped out before, I was most definitely scared now.

"Marleigh, you're creeping me out," I told her.

There was nothing to come from her mouth. Complete silence filled the room. Slowly she lifted her hand and signaled for me to follow her. Her pace was even slower. I made sure to keep my distance because I wasn't sure if this was Marleigh or the poltergeist, but I didn't want any parts. Smoke filled the room until eventually everything around us was black.

"Your future," Marleigh spoke in the most chilling tone.

When the air cleared, I stood there standing in front of my club. Looking around, I couldn't believe my eyes. Anger and rage filled me as the business that I had built to perfection looked like a broken-down trap house.

"What in the hell happened?" I mumbled and walked towards the entrance of the club.

When I entered the club, the smell of stale Black- N-Milds filled the air. Placing my hand over my nose, another rancid smell of mold and urine hit me. I wanted to gag. Walking through the club, I couldn't believe my eyes. It was nothing but bums in here.

"This can't be life."

I sighed as I neared the bar and an older woman stood behind it. Lord, she was pouring Club Cocktails into red Solo cups. In a rage, I walked off, and in the far corner, it was a group of older men engaged in a card game.

"Where the hell am I because I just know I didn't run my shit in the ground like this?" I yelled, damn near in tears.

When I got closer to the back, I spotted Ced. What was he doing here? He looked nice and out of his element.

"Ms. Wanda, I need two rooms in the back," he called out to the older lady. She nodded her head. Now, I know they didn't turn this into no hoe house.

Following him to the back, I watched as he entered what used to be a private lounge. There were a few girls in there, and they were bagging up dope. All I could do was shake my head. I couldn't ask Marleigh shit because she was a mute, and I couldn't see to save my soul how all this happened. I didn't work this hard for this to be the outcome.

"Yo, boss, I got that for you."

I turned around to another person entering the room. What I saw brought tears to my eyes. It was Marissa's older son Darius. Ced dapped him up and took the money from him.

"You good? You get your siblings situated?" Ced asked Darius.

"Yeah, everything is everything. I really appreciate you helping me out with this little job because ever since moms died, it's been hard as hell on us," Darius told him. I turned to Marleigh.

"What happened to Marissa?" I asked. She continued to be mute, pissing me off. Walking over to her, I got in her face.

"What happened to Marissa?" I asked through gritted teeth.

Marleigh lifted her finger and pointed to the TV mounted on the wall. A news reporter stood there as Marissa's picture flashed across the screen.

"Prostitute found dead off of Brick Church Pike today," the lady spoke, and I couldn't hear anymore.

I walked out of the room and realized I was crying. Taking a seat, I had to take in all of what just happened. Feeling a tap on my shoulders, I looked up into Marleigh's dark black eyes. She lifted her arm slowly, and smoke started to form. She walked towards the smoke and looked back at me. Rolling my eyes, I got up and followed behind her.

As we walked through the dark cloud, I started to see something ahead of me, but I couldn't make it out. Squinting my eyes, I was really trying to see through this thick smoke. Marleigh stopped, and she moved to the side, clearing the view. There before me was a black casket. I wasn't sure what it was that Marleigh wanted me to see, so I turned around behind me, and we were in an empty church. Not a single soul was in the room. Turning back to face the casket, there now stood a huge portrait of myself. Shaking my head, I knew this couldn't be what I thought it was, so I walked closer to the casket. Slowly I lifted the lid and was looking at my own face. My pale face had a permanent mug on there. Damn, a bitch didn't even die happy.

Looking at myself lying there lifeless was killing me slowly. Why was there nobody here to see me be put away? I turned back around, and rage filled me.

"Why is nobody here?" I yelled.

"You mean to tell me all the money I had y'all couldn't pay a motherfucker to come see me? Where is Bambino? If anybody should be here, should be him!" I cried.

The doors of the church opened, and two men in suits walked in.

"That's more like it," I mumbled. They walked over to the casket and closed the lid.

"I don't think as long as I ever worked in this business nobody showed up for a funeral. She's been out here all day and not one visit," he said.

"Word around town she was one of them stuck up ass money-hungry women. It's sad she got robbed at the ATM. Whoever took that had a nice payday," the other man said.

"I don't see why she was walking around with that much money on her anyway. She was asking for it."

I stood there mouth wide listening to them carry on about me. Hearing I was robbed, which led me to my demise, was somewhat not shocking. Bambino always would tell me not to carry that much money around on me like that at one time. Watching them carry me out of the church and put me in the back of a hearse was something I never envisioned. I was speechless for the first time in my life.

Marleigh and I followed them to my burial site, and once we got there, it was even eerie than the funeral. Not a soul was there besides the dead that was already there. Once my burial was complete, I stood motionless over the freshly laid dirt. It was safe to say that I didn't love enough for anyone to love me. I hurt a lot of people and damaged some that could've had something great for them.

A cold feeling started to take over me, and my body grew cold as I walked around the plot. The grass held a dewy glaze even in the middle of the day. In the distance, I could see Marleigh watching. I took a deep breath inhaling the fresh air. Even though death was all around, it was peaceful and pleasant. All the other graves had beautiful tombstones, and I wasn't sure how mine would turn out, seeing that I had no one now.

I kneeled towards the dirt and placed my hand on the moist soil. If nobody cried for me, I did. A feeling of doom came over me, and I looked at Marleigh pointing to a dark cloud. Standing up, I looked back at my grave one last time before walking off.

Walking through the dark mist, I was hoping nothing bad happened to Bambino because why wasn't he at my funeral, and why did he let my club go to shit and basically turned into a damn trap house.

When the mist cleared, Marleigh led me down a long corridor in which her black dress trailed behind her. Looking at the doors, I realized we were at the hospital. Instantly I felt my heart beating in my throat. Marleigh stopped at a closed door and slowly lifted her arm pointing to the door.

When I took a closer look at Marleigh, I noticed her face had deteriorated. She was the presence of death, and slowly her body was displaying that. There was nothing I could say or do, so I walked towards the door and turned the knob entering the room. Bambino sat in a chair beside the bed with his head in his hands. When I looked at the bed, Ti'Miya laid there peacefully. Walking over the machines that she was hooked up to, I realized they weren't on.

"Oh no, please tell me she isn't gone?" I asked Marleigh. She never said a word.

Racing over to Bam, I kneeled in front of him, knowing that he couldn't see me, but I wanted to touch him so bad. I wanted to comfort him if what I was looking at was true.

Finally, he lifted his head, and his eyes were bloodshot red. He stood up and walked over to Ti'Miya and placed his hand on her forehead.

"Daddy's so sorry that he failed you. I don't even know what to do now without you. I have no purpose to keep on. It isn't fair. I just want to trade places with you," he cried.

The door opened, and a doctor entered the room.

"Mr. Kratchit, we have to take her now," he said sadly.

Bam planted a million kisses on Ti'Miya's forehead, and his tears wet her face. As the nurses came in to roll the bed out of the room, Bambino never let go. I followed behind him as they walked to the morgue. The further we walked, we came to a point where we couldn't cross. The doctor held his hand up in front of Bam.

"This is far as we can let you follow. Someone will be with you shortly to get your arrangements for a funeral home," he told him.

Bambino stood there, but I couldn't stop. I continued through the doors right beside her. Precious Ti'Miya was an innocent life that didn't want for much. Why did she have to face this? This hurts worse than seeing myself dead.

"I'm going to be ok," a little voice startled me.

Turning around, Ti'Miya stood behind me. I looked back at the bed at her peaceful face, which looked as if she was sleeping. When I felt a little hand slip inside of mine, I squeezed it.

"I'm so sorry, Ti'Miya," I mumbled. This was new to me. I didn't know if I should hug her or what. Ti'Miya smiled.

"I told you it's ok," she said again. This time I felt that gloomy feeling coming back, and Ti'Miya turned to face Marleigh's ghost. Marleigh held her arm out for Ti'Miya to grab.

"Now where are you going?" I shouted. Ti'Miya kept walking into Marleigh's arm until she disappeared.

The room started spinning rapidly, and I could vividly see my funeral, Bambino crying, the outcome of my club, and flashes of Marleigh before her death and the smile that graced my face whenever we were together. It was like I was being haunted by everything that took place over the years. Placing my hands on the side of my head, I tried to drown out the voices.

"I always loved you, but I will never forgive you," Bambino's voice echoed.

"You need to get your life together," Marleigh's voiced trailed.

"It's going to be ok," Ti'Miya angelic voice echoed as well.

All of a sudden, everything came to a complete halt. There I stood face-to-face with Bambino. At least I thought we were face-to-face, but I was the other side of the mirror he was looking in. Bam had never looked like this before, and it was almost as if I didn't know him. He had fallen completely off. His locs that he always kept done were matted to his head. It was sure that he hadn't shaved in months. As he looked at his reflection, his eyed carried a distance about them as if he wasn't entirely there. When he lifted his hand, he was holding a gun.

Immediately I started shaking my head no. Placing the gun to his head, Bambino opened his mouth to speak.

"I guess all of us will be together now. Marleigh, Eboneigh, Ti'Miya, and me," he mumbled as a single tear rolled down his face.

At the sound of the gunshot and me screaming, I felt myself falling. Trying to grab hold of something, my arms were flying everywhere as if I was trapped underwater and couldn't come up.

Chapter 11
Eboneigh

"Ahh!" I shouted as I gasped for air and my eyes opened.

The sun was beaming through the curtains so bright that I turned my head. I quickly scanned the room realizing I was back home. I grabbed my phone and checked the date, and it was December 25th. The time was six a.m., and I had a long day ahead of me. Swinging my feet around, I hopped out of bed and did a little stretch dance.

"Alexa play "Silent Night" by The Temptations". I smiled.

As soon as the music came through my bedroom speakers, a smile spread across my face. Feeling my chest, I touched the necklace that Marleigh had given me many years ago.

"Thank you for waking me up, friend. I should have never left this earth when you left because that hurt me something awful. I never knew my body was here, but my soul left right along with you. Thank God for a wake-up call. I'm glad to know that I have you as an angel, sis." I smiled.

As the sounds of The Temptations filled the room, I headed in my closet and grabbed my red off the shoulder sweater, a pair of denim jeans, and my red thigh-high boots. Once I laid all of my clothing out, I had to make a few calls to some important people. I knew it was Christmas day, and many places were closed, but let's just say in my line of business my clientele of regulars weren't basic people.

I pulled out my iPad and started to go through my list of things to do, and after an hour, I had completed all my calls, and everything was turning out perfect. As the Christmas tunes continued to play, I headed to the bathroom to handle my hygiene.

While in the shower, I hummed along to the tunes, and I could feel the positive energy flowing through my veins. Ain't no way in hell I was going back to the Eboneigh that I once was. The cold and callous Eboneigh was dead and gone. I left her in that old world. I had hearts to mend and people to love on.

As soon as I finished showering, I got dressed and grabbed my mink coat. Walking through the house, it was so cold and not welcoming of Christmas. This would be the last time my house would feel like this. Hell, the way I was feeling, I would decorate year-round because I had a lot of making up to do.

Leaving my condo, I drove to my first destination. On my ride there, I had to drive in silence because this visit was about to be life-changing. I wasn't sure of the outcome, and that scared me.

"God, I know I was wrong for the way I handled this, but I'm here now to change. Fault me for not being guided and giving up instead of trying," I said aloud.

I turned into Target parking lot and pulled around to the side and sent a text to the guy that I had spoken to earlier. He was the manager here and a regular at the club. Stepping outside, I popped the trunk and made my way around to the back, where he loaded my trunk with the things I had asked for.

"I really appreciate you doing this for me because you didn't have to." I smiled.

"It's nothing Eboneigh. Here you're going to need this," he said, holding out a red Santa hat. Grabbing the hat, I smiled and placed it on my head.

"Thank you again," I told him. We shook hands, and he walked off. I stopped halfway back and turned around.

"Merry Christmas!" I yelled out.

Clapping my hands in excitement, I got back in the car and headed in the direction of my first stop. I had the heat on blast because it was cold as hell outside. Looking at the time on the dash, it was almost eight o'clock.

Pulling up at the house that I remembered vividly in my visit, I cut the engine off and sat there for a minute. Closing my eyes, I did a few breathing exercises to ease the butterflies in my stomach.

"There's no turning back now," I said.

Looking in the mirror, I made sure the hat sat right on my head and got out of the car. Making my way to the door, I could feel my palms getting sweaty as cold as it was outside. Shaking it off, I pressed the doorbell. When I went to press the bell again, the door flew open, and Bambino looked at me like I was crazy. He wore a shocked look on his face.

"Merry Christmas!" I smiled.

He looked at me from head to toe taking me all in. The energy between us was so magnetic that I gravitated towards him and hugged him as tight as I could. I could feel the hesitancy, and finally, he wrapped his arms around me.

"I'm so sorry for the way I've treated you all these years, Bam. I have always loved you. I just didn't know how to show you, and when Marleigh died, I didn't want to be loved. Most importantly, I'm sorry for."

"Mommy!" Ti'Miya yelled as she came from behind Bambino.

We pulled apart, and I wiped the tears from my eyes as I wrapped arms around my child. Lord Jesus, I haven't held her since birth. I sat down right there in the doorway and just held my child.

"See daddy, Santa listens," she said. Cupping my hands around her face, I looked into her eyes.

"Mommy will never leave your side again, and we're going to get you well," I told her. Looking up at Bambino, he was crying and smiling at the same time.

"Can you go get all that stuff out of my trunk please," I told him. He nodded his head.

Ti'Miya and I got up and headed to the living room, which was filled with gift paper everywhere from her opening gifts already. After Marleigh's death, I had completely shut down and put all my energy into building the club and pushing for it to be the best. Hiring Bam as my assistant, he stayed by my side like he has been most of my life. We have been fucking on and off since I was thirteen. I just never wanted a relationship with him.

When I found out I was pregnant with Ti'Miya, I was livid. I didn't have a motherly bone in my body. I didn't want a child, and my business was at its peak. Bambino didn't want me to get rid of the baby and vowed that he would raise his child regardless if I wanted any parts. What hurt me the most was after I had her, I thought the motherly feeling would kick in, but it never did. I felt a disconnect I blame that on my upbringing and my own mom.

Bam walked back into the house and placed all the bags in front of the tree. Ti'Miya eyes lit up like the tree.

"Can I talk to you for a second?" Bam asked, breaking me from my thoughts.

I stood up from the couch and followed him to the kitchen. He leaned up against the counter and placed his hand under his chin like he was contemplating what to say.

"Look, I don't know what prompted this change, and I'm all for it, but I'm telling you now don't hurt her, EB," he said in a serious tone. It was understandable, and I didn't feel a way or get angry.

"Listen, let's just say last night was a very long night for me and not an ordinary one. I had a chance to think really see things for what they are. I would never pop in her life to get her this excited and then leave. If I have to take parenting classes, I will, but I want to be the best mother and give her something that I never had. She deserves that and more. I reached out to her doctor via-email, and Monday morning I'm going in for testing so that I can see if I can be a donor. How come you never told me she was having problems?" I asked.

"EB, you're not the easiest to talk to about her. You walk around here as if she literally never existed."

Bam stepped closer to me and grabbed my hands.

"So does this mean we can be a family and finally be together?" he whispered.

"Yeah, that's exactly what it means, BK." I winked. He frowned up.

"Don't even bother lying. I know about your little operation you and Ced got. One thing though, if anything ever happens to me, you bet not turn my club into no damn broke down trap house," I said, hitting him in his arm.

"How in the hell you know all this?" he asked.

"It doesn't matter, I know." I laughed. Bam leaned in, and we let our lips touch as we shared a kiss. Placing my arms around his neck, I didn't want this to end.

"Come on. Ti'Miya done got too quiet." He laughed as he pulled me back towards the living room.

I took a seat next to Ti'Miya and helped her opened her gifts.

Chapter 12
Bambino

I tossed and turned most of the night because I had so much weighing on my mind, and the energy was just off, so when I finally drifted off to sleep, Ti'Miya came rushing in the room ready to open gifts. I still bought her some things even though it was clear what she wanted. Pulling myself from the bed, we headed to the living room where I watched as she opened everything. I prayed she didn't bring up her mom or the kidney because I didn't want to hurt her feelings.

While Ti'Miya was playing, the doorbell rang, and I was expecting no type of company. When I opened that door and saw Eboneigh standing there all bright-eyed and full of smiles, that shit scared me. The things she was saying I had waited my whole life to hear and for her to get some act right. I wouldn't be the man I am if I didn't pull her to the side and question where this was coming from. I had to look out for Ti'Miya. I didn't want her getting her hopes up and then get her heartbroken because EB ups and decides she doesn't want to be mommy anymore.

I sat off to the side and watched how they interacted and was thankful for this change. I had my girl and my family. To hear that she was going to take the steps to find out if she could be a donor was everything a nigga needed to hear. I wasn't going to stop fighting for my daughter. Ti'Miya never gave up hope on her mom even though, at times, I wasn't so sure.

"Hey, I have a few stops that I need to make today, and I was wondering if you guys would like to tag along?" EB walked over and asked me.

"It's a holiday, EB. What you got to do on Christmas?" I asked.

"I'm still in the process of correcting some wrongs. I have to do this today, so are you guys coming? I have a surprise back at my house for both of you as well." She smiled.

I didn't know what she had up her sleeve, but I couldn't say no to this new EB.

"Cool, let me get us situated," I told her, getting up.

"You can go take care of yourself, and I'll go get Ti'Miya ready," she suggested. I held my hands up in a surrender motion.

"Fine with me," I answered and headed to my room.

***

About an hour later and we were all in EB's car, and she still hadn't told me where we were going. Looking over at her while she was driving, she didn't frown once. It was like her smile was a permanent fixture. Looking in the backseat, Ti'Miya sat busy on her tablet, paying us no mind.

"Guess what movie we watched last night?" I looked back at EB and asked.

"Our Christmas tradition movie," EB answered and smiled.

"I swear I feel like you were peeping in a nigga window or something."

"You can say that. You know I haven't watched that movie since Marleigh. I think I might have to dust it off." She shrugged. EB rarely spoke on Marleigh, so this was a first.

As soon as we turned into the subdivision, I knew where we were going. My antenna went up.

"Why we at Marissa's house, EB? You know how the two of y'all rock," I asked. They hated each other, and I didn't feel like being in the middle of any bullshit.

"Chill, it's nothing like you're probably thinking in your head. Come on," EB reassured me, and we got out.

I grabbed Ti'Miya out of the car and followed EB to the door saying a silent prayer.

Chapter 13
Eboneigh

My next stop was to see Marissa. When I knocked on her door, I wasn't so sure what direction this was going to go in because she was a hothead like me.

"Who is it?" a boy voice could be heard, which I assume was Darius.

"Eboneigh," I answered.

I turned around to look at Bam because there was a delay and I could hear some commotion from behind the door. The door flew open, and Marissa stood there with her hands on her hip and the meanest mug.

"You got your nerve showing up here on my doorstep. How the fuck you know where I live?" she snapped.

It took everything in me not to snap, but I had to remember why I was here and that I also had my child.

"Merry Christmas, Marissa. Is it ok if my family and I come in? It's rather cold out here?" I asked. She looked at Bambino and Ti'Miya before she moved to the side to let us in.

"Now what?" she spat.

"You have every right to be hostile with me because I know I'm the last person you want to see. Considering my child is right here, can you be a little calmer. I'm not here to be disrespectful, and I don't want to show such distaste in front of her.

"When did you have a kid? When did this happen?" she laughed, pointing to Bambino and me.

"Let me get straight to the reason that I'm here so that I can get out of your hair." I smiled.

"First, I want to apologize for firing you yesterday. I come to realize I have been what you call unpleasant to work for. Not that it's an excuse for my behavior, but I let me being damaged run the way I treat others, and that isn't right. I never cared to learn that someone else might be going through something just as bad as me. I see that you are raising four beautiful children alone, and I have some things I would like to offer you," I told her.

Reaching into my bag, I pulled out a few envelopes.

"It's time that you make your house a home, so I called my friend at Rooms To Go, and you can go out there and get whatever you need to furnish your house, and I mean everything."

"Are you serious?" Marissa asked.

"Inside this envelope is a check to cover your kid's tuition for the remainder of the school year. As far as your job, we're going to find you something to your liking. I have spoken with some friends that are willing to hire you. You are more than that pole." I smiled.

By this time, Marissa was ugly crying, and her kids were smiling. Darius stood off to the side. He even had a smile on his face.

"Oh my god, EB! I don't know what came over you, but I just want to hug you right now."

"I've placed some money in your bank account to cover your expenses until your income from your new job starts rolling in because the kids still need things and got to eat. As my last surprise for you, I wouldn't be really changed if I didn't do it. My daughter is sick, and I don't know what it's like to take care of someone in that nature where everything relies on you. You don't have to worry about your Mee-

Maw's medical expenses or medicine because I got it covered." Marissa grabbed me and placed me in the tightest hug.

"I'm sorry that we always used to butt heads, and I called you everything but a child of God. I don't know how I could ever repay you for this, but thank you for helping keep the light of my family's eyes. I almost felt like I let them down," she admitted.

I felt her tears hitting my shoulders, and I rubbed her back because I was crying as well.

"Your strength is amazing, and I guess that's why we never got along because you didn't ever take my shit. I just want you to not ever have to resort to doing anything low for cash. I don't want you stripping unless that's just something you want to do. Speaking of the club," I said, pulling away from her and turning to Bambino.

"I have an announcement to make. Effective immediately, we are no longer a twenty-four club. We will only be open Thursday, Fridays, and Saturdays. Now the remainder days, I will still run as a restaurant and lounge, but we will run normal business hours. That means less of me around the club because my focus is on Ti'Miya." I looked at her and winked.

"Wow, I just thought of something. You can manage the club during the week," I told Marissa. Her mouth dropped.

"I would love to, but back it up because you keep avoiding the elephant in the room. When did this become a thing?" Marissa said, pointing to Bam and me once again.

"This has been a thing since we were thirteen, and I've been playing with his heart all these years. I could talk forever on this man's greatness, but I messed up big time when it came to my child, so I just want to focus on being the best mommy I can be because I have no clue how to do this." I laughed, but it was the painful truth.

"You got this, EB. It will come naturally now that you're open to it. I bet you already love her more than life itself, right?" Marissa asked, lifting her brow.

I thought about what Marissa said and how when I first hugged Ti'Miya, I didn't want to let her go.

"You know what I really do," I admitted.

"This has turned out to be a great Christmas," Marissa cheered.

"I'm glad I could assist. I have one more stop to make before I head home, but call me whenever you need anything and take you a holiday break. I'll see you after the new year to get you trained for that manager position," I smiled.

Marissa hugged me again, and I waved bye to her kids.

Once we got settled and warm in the car, I felt Bam staring a hole in me. Looking at him, I turned to face him.

"Why are you looking at me like that?" I asked. Bam leaned closer to me and picked up my hand.

"I ain't gone lie. I was scared back there. I was like Lord. It's about to go down with these two together. What you did for her was awesome because that girl be struggling. She just wanted something good for her kids and took them out of the hood. I would help her every now and then it's good to see that your heart ain't made of stone. Honestly, that turned me on. I love you, Eboneigh," Bam whispered.

"I love you too, Bambino." Giving him a quick peck on the lips, I put the car in reverse and headed to our next stop.

***

"When was the last time you been here?" Bam stood close to me, trying to keep me warm.

"I haven't been here since we buried her. You know for the longest, I was so mad at her because I felt she shouldn't have ever gone to see his ass. I just kept thinking about our last moments together and then that phone call. When we buried her, I went right along with her." Slowly, I reached for the necklace around my neck and touched it.

"Marleigh came to me in my dreams, and she was pissed. She had to have me look at my life from a different view, and that shit woke me up, Bam. That shit was terrible just to know I've been down here being a disappointment to her this entire time. Marleigh's always looked out for me even in death," I told him.

Looking at her tombstone, I kneeled close to the ground.

"Marleigh, thank you for everything and thank you for being the best sister and friend a girl could ever ask for. You can stop your bitching because we're together now too." I laughed, looking back at Bambino.

"Yeah, sis, we together now, and thank you for giving me my baby back." He laughed. I kissed her stone and then kissed my necklace.

"Merry Christmas, Marleigh!" I sang.

Bam placed his arms around me, and we walked a few steps to the car. Ti'Miya was knocked out, taking a little nap, so we left her in the car.

"So, Santa where to now?" Bam joked.

"To my house for my last surprise," I smiled.

Right when I was about to pull off, the radio started playing "Silent Night" by The Temptations. Bam and I both looked at each other with a smirk on our faces.

"It's safe to say that Marleigh heard everything we said back there," I laughed. That was a sign from nobody but her.

Chapter 14
Eboneigh

Getting off the elevator, we walked in the direction of my place. Bam was holding Ti'Miya. My insides started to flutter because I prayed what I envisioned and planned came out perfectly. When I opened the door to my place, Ti'Miya's voice instantly echoed with wows. Bam put her down as he took in everything, and I must say the décor was everything. While I was gone, I had my decorator come and decorate my house with everything Christmas.

"Merry Christmas you guys!" I cheered.

We removed our coats, and I headed straight to the kitchen. It was now after noon, and I still had time to prepare us something to eat. It wasn't about being in a hurry to eat. I just wanted to spend this time with my family and hopefully, start our own traditions.

"What you about to burn up?" Bam came in the kitchen and placed his arms around my waist.

"First of all, I might not cook, but you know I can get down, so don't even play me like that," I told him. Reaching into the fridge, I pulled out the steaks that I had in there.

"It was a little short notice to make a real Christmas meal, but I'm going to make it do what it do with what I got in here." I smiled.

"You want me to do anything?" he asked.

"Pour me a glass of wine and go sit back and relax," I demanded him.

I cleaned the steaks and seasoned them. Placing them in the skillet, I then browned the steak and set them in the oven for a bit. While the steaks were in the oven, I grabbed some spinach and sautéed them in garlic and butter. Grabbing some carrots from the fridge, I sliced them up and seasoned so that I could make some glazed carrots. While the rest of my dinner continued to cook, I set the table.

Grabbing my glass of wine, I stood off to the side, looked in the living room, and just quietly watched Ti'Miya and Bam interact. Shaking my head, I couldn't believe I turned this down. The feeling of emptiness I used to have was now full and overflowing.

"Dinner will be ready in a minute. You guys can go get cleaned up," I told them, finishing off my glass.

Making my way back to the kitchen, I removed everything and placed them in serving dishes, sitting them on the dining table. It's crazy I had never used this table. Looking at everything, I was satisfied. Bam and Ti'Miya made their way into the dining area, and we took our seats.

"This looks good, baby," Bam smiled.

"Thank you, I'll say grace," I told him. Bam nodded his head as we bowed our heads.

"Dear Heavenly Father, love brought Jesus to the earth, and love brings us to this table. Today as we share this holiday meal, may we also share with each other a joyful heart and a warm smile. May our Christmas dinner be filled with love and kindness, and may the memories of today warm our hearts for years to come. Amen,"

"Amen," Bam and Ti'Miya said in unison.

"Let's eat!" Bam said, rubbing his hands together. We chowed down and joy-filled the room as we laughed and embraced being together.

Dinner was complete, and Bam was cleaning the kitchen while Ti'Miya and I sat in the living room, painting our nails with our pajamas on. We were on chill mode for the rest of the day and not doing anything.

"Mommy, I'm so glad you came back," she said. That mommy word had a nice ring to it.

"I'm glad I'm back too, baby. The next thing we're going to do is get you better," I reassured her. Bam came into the room.

"What are my two favorite girls doing?" he asked, standing behind me.

"Getting all dolled up, you know we got to stay fly," I told him.

"Well, I think you might need this to be fly." I turned around, and he stood there, holding out a velvet box.

"What the hell is that?" I asked him. He kneeled to my level and opened the box.

"I've been holding on to this for a long time, and I would pray that one day you would come around and let me love you fully. We've been knowing each other for about twelve years, and hell, we got a kid together. I just hope now since you're letting me love you, could you let me love you even more by being my wife?" he asked.

The tears were falling, and I was ugly crying.

"You know, I will!" I cried. Bam slid the ring on my finger, and I fell into his arms.

"I knew I loved you when you were thirteen when I bought your ass all that shit." He smiled. Ti'Miya climbed in my lap, and I looked at my ring. This was what it was all about.

Epilogue
Eboneigh

Five Months Later

The doctor entered the room, reading over his paperwork. I prayed he was about to deliver good news. Out of habit and being nervous, I reached over and grabbed Bambino's hand. He squeezed my hand, and I knew that meant it was going to be okay.

"So, after looking over all the test results and labs, the kidney is functioning extremely well to Ti'Miya's body. She isn't showing any signs of the earlier symptoms she possessed before treatment. How have things been going for you Ms. Scroo?" he asked me.

"I've actually been better. I thought with me having one kidney, my pregnancy would be somewhat tough, but since I'm over the early part of it, I actually feel great." I shrugged.

I was four months pregnant with Bam and my second child.

"That's good, but people live healthy even with one kidney. I want to see Ti'Miya back in a few months just to continue to check-in and make sure everything is fine. However, from the looks of it, all her kidney problems are over."

"Thank you, Doc," Bambino told him. We gathered our things and left the doctor's office.

Right after Christmas, I immediately went to the doctor and started the process that I needed to take in order to be a donor for Ti'Miya. Once they told me that my kidney was approved for the transplant within two weeks, we were having surgery. I wasn't about to play with my child's life.

During our healing process, I stayed home while Bam ran his operation and helped trained Marissa while making the changes I wanted for the club. Within that time, Bam's horny ass got me pregnant.

Things at the club were turning out better than I envisioned. Marissa took her job seriously, and the way she was running the club and taking care of home was that of a boss. The money was good, and everyone was happy. I was even looking at new business ventures for the future. There is always money to be made.

Bam and I were planning a summer wedding, but with me being pregnant, I didn't want to get married until after I had the baby because I was about to go all out for my wedding dress, and this stomach wasn't going to let me be great, so we opted for the following spring instead. I guess it's safe to say life is great, and I'm forever embracing change.

The End

Thank You

Thank you for reading book 19, and I really hope you enjoyed this spin of a Christmas classic. It's one of my all-time favorite Christmas stories. If you can, please leave a review good or bad. I would also like to wish everyone a Merry Christmas and a Happy Holidays. Embrace your loved ones while they're here and love each other because tomorrow is never promised.

Kyeate's Catalog

Games He Play: Di'mond & Kyng

A Savage and his Lady (Series 1& 2)

Masking My Pain

Fiyah & Desire: Down to ride for a Boss

Securing the Bag and His Heart (Series)

Securing the Bag and His Heart Too

Remnants (Novella)

5 Miles Until Empty (Novella)

Once Upon a Hood Love: A Nashville Fairytale (Novella)

Tricked: A Halloween Love Story (Novella)

Kali Kusain: Counterfeit Queen

Dear Saint Nik: A Christmas Novella

My First Night with You: A BWWM Novella

Enticed by a Cold-Hearted Menace

Me vs. Me: Life of Deceit

Her Mended Soul

Taking a Thug's Love

Valuable Pain: Money, Lies, & Heartbreak

CPSIA information can be obtained
at www.ICGtesting.com
Printed in the USA
LVHW111806070120
642793LV00003B/431/P

9 781672 946797